This Little Tiger book belongs to:

_____

_____

_____

For Scarlet who is also very good at sharing porridge! ~ S S

For Sam – you know why! ~ T W

LITTLE TIGER PRESS
1 The Coda Centre,
189 Munster Road, London SW6 6AW
www.littletiger.co.uk

First published in Great Britain 2011
This edition published 2012
Text copyright © Steve Smallman 2011
Illustrations copyright © Tim Warnes 2011
Visit Tim Warnes at www.ChapmanandWarnes.com
Steve Smallman and Tim Warnes have asserted their rights
to be identified as the author and illustrator of this work
under the Copyright, Designs and Patents Act, 1988
A CIP catalogue record for this book
is available from the British Library
All rights reserved

ISBN 978-1-84895-133-4
LTP/1900/0883/0314
Printed in China
2 4 6 8 10 9 7 5 3

Icky Little Duckling

Steve Smallman   Tim Warnes

LITTLE TIGER PRESS
London

Mr Rabbit liked everything to be **just so**:
every flower, **just so**, every pebble, **just so**,
every leaf in the forest perfectly neat —
and **just so**!

One day, he was busy tidying when he found something smooth and speckly and perfect. "Oh my whiskers!" he gasped. "You're just the thing for my collection!"

Mr Rabbit hurried home. He carefully
washed the perfect, speckly thing and placed it,
just so, in the middle of his collection.

He loved it. He often sat,
polishing it and humming
a happy little hum.

But then, one evening, CRACK!
a jagged line appeared down the side
of Mr Rabbit's perfect, speckly thing.

"Oh my whiskers!"
he gasped in horror. "Don't worry!
We'll soon have you mended!"

But it was too late.

CRACK!

it broke in two…

…and out came something icky,
sticky and strange. Not **just so** at all.
It looked up at Mr Rabbit
and said…"**Mama!**"

Mama!

"What?!" cried Mr Rabbit.
"No, no, no, I am *not* your..."

"**Mama!**" it said again,
even louder.

Then it hopped onto
the floor, grabbed hold
of Mr Rabbit's leg and
wouldn't let go.

"Yuck!" groaned Mr Rabbit. He popped the icky, sticky thing into a big, bubbly bath. "First, you must be clean! We'll find your 'mama' in the morning."

quack!

Soon there were bubbles on the floor, bubbles on Mr Rabbit, and bubbles all over the burrow!

"Goodness me!" gasped Mr Rabbit. "You're a duckling!"

Gurgle-urgle-urgle! went the duckling's stomach.
"Oh, bother," grumbled Mr Rabbit. "*Now* you're hungry.
Erm... do you like porridge?"

The little duckling *did* like porridge.

She liked to sit in it…

she liked to splash in it…

and she liked to share it
with Mr Rabbit!
"Yeeeuck!" groaned
Mr Rabbit and he filled
up the bath again.

Mama!

"Yawn!" went the little duckling.
  "Bedtime, thank goodness!"
cried Mr Rabbit.
"Soon be morning!"

He popped the duckling
into a box and tucked
her in, **just so**.

Mama?

But the duckling didn't
stay **just so** for long…

Mr Rabbit flopped into his chair.
"What a mess!" he groaned.
"I'll tidy it up in the...

zZZ ZzZZ!"

"Mama?" whispered the little
duckling. She scrambled onto
Mr Rabbit's lap, snuggled up
and fell fast asleep too.

Next morning, they set off to find the duckling's 'mama'.

Duckling found
a stretchy thing…

and some spotty bugs.

Then she found a grumpy old
prickle monster and had to have
a hug from Mr Rabbit.
But they didn't find
her 'mama'.

Back at home, Mr Rabbit made some more porridge. The duckling found lots of lovely things to play with!

"Put those down!"
shouted Mr Rabbit. "Carefully!
Oh I hope we find your
'mama' soon!" he sighed.

But they didn't find her the next day.
Or the day after that.

Then, one morning, down beside the stream, the duckling shouted, "**Mama!**" And this time, she was right!

She leapt to meet her family in a happy huddle of kisses and quacks.

Then as Mr Rabbit turned to leave,
the little duckling jumped into his arms and
gave him a great, big, feathery hug.

"Thank you so much, Mr Rabbit!"
said Mrs Duck.

Back in his burrow, Mr Rabbit scrubbed and polished until everything was as neat as before.

His books were **just so**.
His boxes were **just so**.
And his collection was
tip-top, totally **just so**.

But he didn't feel right. Everything was **just so** but he was just so… lonely. Even his special things didn't seem so special any more.

Then Mr Rabbit had a wonderful idea…
"**Oh my whiskers!**" he cried.
"I'll need lots of porridge!"

Mr Rabbit invited the duck family to tea.
His burrow didn't stay neat for long but it was filled
with giggles and quacks and fun and friends.
And Mr Rabbit thought it was **just perfect!**

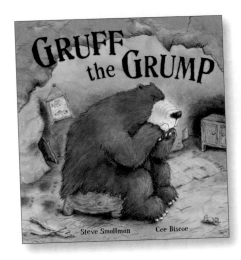

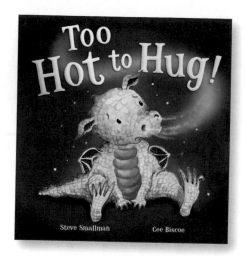

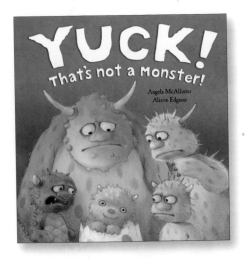

Books from Little Tiger that are just perfect!

For information regarding any of the above titles or for our catalogue, please contact us:
Little Tiger Press, 1 The Coda Centre, 189 Munster Road, London SW6 6AW
Tel: 020 7385 6333 • Fax: 020 7385 7333 • E-mail: contact@littletiger.co.uk • www.littletiger.co.uk